THE REVERSE GAME

Tammy Simmons

Copyright © 2024 Tammy Simmons

All rights reserved

The characters and events portrayed in this book are fictitious. Any similarity to real persons, living or dead, is coincidental and not intended by the author.

No part of this book may be reproduced, or stored in a retrieval system, or transmitted in any form or by any means, electronic, mechanical, photocopying, recording, or otherwise, without express written permission of the publisher.

ISBN-13: 9798301048692

Cover design by: Tammy Simmons
Library of Congress Control Number: 2018675309
Printed in the United States of America

CONTENTS

CHAPTER ONE

The sun beat down on the blacktop, baking the concrete beneath Dominic's sneakers as he dribbled the ball in rhythm. The squeak of rubber soles echoed in the small city park, punctuated by the occasional curse or laughter from his crew. Dominic was in his element, weaving through defenders with ease, a smirk tugging at the corner of his lips. This was his court, his kingdom, and today was no different.

Sean's booming voice cut through the noise. "Come on, Dom, quit showboating!" he yelled, tossing a quick glance toward the sideline where his girlfriend, Tiana, had just arrived. She wasn't alone.

Dominic's eyes flickered over mid-play. Tiana was waving, her usual radiant smile plastered across her face, but it was the woman standing beside her that caught his attention. She had long braids pulled back into a loose ponytail, dark skin glowing in the sunlight, and an effortless elegance that didn't belong on a basketball court.

"Who's that?" Dominic muttered to Sean as the ball bounced out of bounds.

Sean followed his gaze, grinning. "That's Vanessa. Tiana's friend. Try not to scare her off, alright?"

Dominic rolled his eyes but didn't respond. He grabbed the ball and jogged to the sidelines, tossing it to Malik. "Finish the game without me," he said. His tone was casual, but his focus was locked.

Vanessa didn't notice Dominic approaching at first, too engrossed in a conversation with Tiana. He stood there a moment, taking her in—how she tilted her head slightly when she laughed, the soft cadence of her voice. For someone who didn't usually think twice about women, Vanessa had an air that held his attention longer than most.

"You two look like you're having fun," Dominic said, flashing a smile as he finally made his presence known.

Vanessa turned, her eyes meeting his. They were a deep, rich brown, framed by lashes that curled naturally. "We are," she said, her voice calm but tinged with curiosity.

"This is Dominic," Tiana offered, gesturing between the two. "Dom, this is Vanessa."

Dominic extended a hand, his grip firm but not overbearing. "Nice to meet you, Vanessa. So, you're here to see me embarrass Sean on the court?"

Vanessa raised an eyebrow, her lips curling into a small smile. "I thought it was supposed to be a team sport."

"With Sean, it's a one-man show," Dominic quipped, earning a laugh from Tiana and a groan from Sean, who was still playing.

The game wrapped up, and before long, the group migrated to Sean's house, a small but cozy space filled with the smell of pepperoni pizza and the sound of laughter. Dominic found himself gravitating toward Vanessa, who was perched on the arm of the couch, nursing a soda.

"So, Vanessa," Dominic said, sliding into the seat beside her. "What do you do when you're not hanging out at basketball courts?"

She tilted her head, studying him for a moment before answering. "I'm an elementary school teacher. And you?"

Dominic leaned back, a playful grin spreading across his face. "I'm a man of many talents. You'll just have to stick around and find out."

"Is that so?" Vanessa's tone was light, but there was a flicker of intrigue in her eyes.

CHAPTER TWO

The night wore on, and the small gathering at Sean's house settled into an easy rhythm. Sean and Tiana were playfully bickering in the kitchen about who had the better jumper, while Malik had his eyes glued to a late-night game on TV. But Dominic barely noticed any of it. His attention stayed on Vanessa.

She was different. Not just in the way she carried herself—graceful but grounded—but in how she held her own in their conversations. No batting of eyelashes or coy responses to stroke his ego. Vanessa answered him straight, almost as if she was challenging him without even trying. It was refreshing, and Dominic found himself leaning in just a little closer every time she spoke.

"So, Mr. Many Talents," Vanessa teased, crossing her legs as she turned to face him. "What exactly are these talents? Or was that just a line?"

Dominic chuckled, the sound low and smooth. "Oh, I've got plenty. Basketball, cooking—"

"Cooking?" she interrupted, arching an eyebrow.

"Don't act so surprised," he said with mock offense. "I make a mean chicken Alfredo."

Vanessa's laughter was soft but genuine. "Sure you do."

"I'll prove it," Dominic said, leaning back confidently. "Dinner at my place. You name the day."

Vanessa hesitated, a flicker of caution crossing her face before she smiled again. "We'll see."

By the time Dominic walked Vanessa to her car that night, there was a noticeable shift between them. The initial banter had softened into something more sincere.

"Thanks for coming out tonight," Dominic said, his usual bravado tempered.

"Thanks for the invite," Vanessa replied. She opened her car door but didn't get in right away. "You're different than I expected."

"How's that?"

"I don't know," she said, tilting her head as if trying to figure him out. "I guess I thought you'd be more...surface-level. But there's more to you, isn't there?"

Dominic felt the words hit him in a place he didn't like to acknowledge. He shrugged it off with a grin. "I'll let you keep guessing."

Vanessa rolled her eyes but smiled. "Goodnight, Dominic."

"Goodnight, Vanessa."

As she drove off, Dominic stood in the glow of the streetlight, watching her taillights disappear down the block. For the first time in a while, he felt a twinge of something he couldn't name.

The following weekend, Vanessa agreed to the dinner. True to his word, Dominic whipped up his signature chicken Alfredo, plating it with surprising finesse for a man who didn't spend much time in the kitchen.

"This is actually good," Vanessa admitted, twirling a forkful of pasta.

"Actually?" Dominic feigned insult. "Did you doubt me?"

"A little," she teased, her smile lighting up the small dining room.

As the night progressed, the conversation took on a more personal tone. Vanessa shared stories about her students, the challenges of teaching, and her dream of one day opening a learning center.

Dominic listened intently, nodding in the right places, but when the conversation shifted toward him, he deflected.

"What about you? What's your dream?" Vanessa asked.

Dominic twirled his fork in the sauce, avoiding her gaze. "I don't really think about stuff like that."

"Why not?"

"I just don't," he said lightly, flashing a quick smile to change the subject. "So, this learning center—what's it gonna look like?"

Vanessa let it slide, but the flicker of curiosity in her eyes told Dominic she'd noticed his dodge.

Later that night, after Vanessa left, Dominic sank into his couch, staring at the half-empty wine glass on the coffee table. Her question lingered in his mind, unsettling him.

What's your dream?

It wasn't that he didn't have one. It was that he didn't believe in it anymore.

CHAPTER THREE

The weeks passed, and Dominic and Vanessa slipped into an easy rhythm. Their dates were never extravagant but always thoughtful—quiet dinners, late-night walks, or lazy afternoons at the park. Dominic had a way of making the simplest moments feel effortless, and Vanessa found herself looking forward to their time together more than she wanted to admit.

“You’re getting too good at this,” Vanessa said one evening as Dominic walked her to her door.

“Too good at what?” he asked, leaning casually against the doorframe.

“At making me laugh,” she said, her voice light but her smile soft.

“Hey, I take my job seriously,” Dominic quipped, but something in the way she looked at him made him pause. Her eyes lingered on his, steady and searching, as if she was trying to peel back a layer he wasn’t ready to show.

“You’re not as smooth as you think you are, Dominic,” Vanessa said, her tone teasing but her gaze unwavering.

He raised an eyebrow, smirking to cover the flicker of unease in his chest. “Oh yeah? What gave me away?”

Vanessa shrugged, unlocking her door. “You let your guard down when you think I’m not looking.” She opened the door but didn’t step inside. “Goodnight, Dominic.”

“Goodnight, Vanessa,” he replied, his smirk faltering as she disappeared inside.

It wasn’t until their fifth date that Dominic noticed the subtle shift. They were sitting on a blanket at the park, a half-eaten pizza box between them, watching the sunset. Vanessa had brought up her family—her mom, who was her biggest supporter, and her younger brother, who was her best friend.

"Do you ever get tired of it?" she asked suddenly, breaking the silence.

"Tired of what?" Dominic replied, glancing over at her.

"Being the guy who always seems like he has it all together," she said.

Dominic laughed softly, leaning back on his elbows. "What makes you think I have it all together?"

"You make it look easy," Vanessa said, her voice softer now. "Like nothing ever really touches you."

Dominic looked at her, the glow of the setting sun casting warm light on her face. For a moment, he thought about telling her the truth—about how the persona he wore like armor wasn't as unbreakable as it seemed. But instead, he smiled.

"That's the trick," he said, his tone playful. "You fake it 'til you make it."

Vanessa laughed, shaking her head. "You're impossible, Dominic."

"Impossible to resist," he teased, earning a roll of her eyes.

At the next basketball game, Sean and Malik couldn't help but comment on how often Dominic was talking about Vanessa.

"Man, you're actually seeing the same girl for more than a week? That's gotta be a record," Sean joked as they took a break on the sidelines.

"Vanessa's cool," Dominic said with a shrug, tossing the ball between his hands.

"Cool enough to settle down?" Malik asked, raising an eyebrow.

"Relax, it's not that serious," Dominic replied quickly, but even as the words left his mouth, they felt hollow.

Sean chuckled. "Better hope she doesn't hear you say that."

Dominic smirked, shooting a perfect three-pointer to end the conversation, but the unease lingered.

Vanessa, on the other hand, was starting to see Dominic as more than just the charismatic guy who knew how to make her laugh.

On one particularly rainy night, he showed up at her place unannounced with soup and a movie when she mentioned she wasn't feeling well.

"Okay, Mr. Chicken Alfredo, did you actually make this?" Vanessa asked, raising an eyebrow at the steaming container.

"I may or may not have called in some reinforcements," Dominic admitted, holding up a takeout bag.

Vanessa laughed, curling up on the couch beside him. "At least you're honest."

"Only sometimes," he said with a grin, but the way he tucked the blanket around her shoulders felt more intimate than playful.

CHAPTER FOUR

Vanessa hadn't planned to fall for Dominic, but it was getting harder to ignore the way he made her feel. He was thoughtful in ways she hadn't expected—a man who knew how to make her laugh until her stomach hurt but also remembered the little things, like how she always ordered extra lemon with her tea.

It wasn't just the grand gestures, like showing up with soup on a rainy night or making her dinner. It was the way he'd listen when she talked about her students or how he'd pull her closer during their late-night walks, as if the world could disappear and it wouldn't matter as long as they had that moment.

She told herself she was taking it slow, but deep down, Vanessa knew she was starting to believe in the idea of them.

One evening, as she sat on her couch scrolling through photos on her phone, Vanessa found herself lingering on a picture Tiana had taken of her and Dominic at the park. They were laughing about something she couldn't even remember now, and the way Dominic looked at her in the photo sent a flutter through her chest.

This is different, she thought, tracing the outline of his smile on the screen.

But even as the thought settled, a small voice in the back of her mind reminded her to be cautious. She'd been in relationships before where things felt perfect at first—until they weren't. And Dominic, for all his charm, wasn't exactly an open book.

He had a way of skirting around questions about himself, redirecting conversations back to her or throwing in a joke to change the subject. At first, she'd found it endearing, but now she wondered if it was something more.

One afternoon, while getting coffee with Tiana, Vanessa brought it up.

"So... Dominic," Vanessa started, stirring her latte.

"What about him?" Tiana asked, leaning back in her chair with a knowing smile.

Vanessa hesitated. "Do you think he's...serious about me?"

Tiana raised an eyebrow. "I mean, he's been seeing you consistently, which is more than I can say for any other girl he's dated. Why? Is he giving you a reason to doubt him?"

"No, not exactly," Vanessa admitted, chewing on her bottom lip. "It's just...sometimes I feel like I'm getting all of him, and other times it's like he's holding something back."

Tiana shrugged. "That's Dominic for you. He's not the easiest guy to figure out, but I've known him a long time. He wouldn't waste his time if he wasn't into you."

Vanessa smiled at the reassurance, but the small knot of doubt in her chest didn't completely unravel.

Still, she chose to believe in him. After all, everyone had their walls, and maybe Dominic just needed more time. She wasn't the type to push. If he wanted to open up, she'd be there.

One night, as they sat on her couch watching a movie, Vanessa found herself leaning her head against Dominic's shoulder. His arm wrapped around her instinctively, pulling her closer, and for a moment, everything felt perfect.

"You're different, you know," she said softly.

"How so?" he asked, his voice low.

Vanessa smiled, looking up at him. "You make me feel safe."

Dominic didn't respond right away, and when he finally spoke, his words were light, almost teasing. "I aim to please."

Vanessa laughed, but as she settled back into his arms, she couldn't shake the feeling that there was more he wasn't saying.

The next morning, Vanessa woke up to a text from Dominic. *Busy day ahead, but thinking of you.*

It was sweet, but something about it felt distant, like he was starting to pull away without actually saying so. She brushed the thought aside, telling herself she was overthinking.

But over the next few weeks, the small things started adding up —shorter texts, postponed plans, and a subtle change in his tone that Vanessa couldn't quite put her finger on.

You're absolutely right, Tammy—this is the perfect moment to transition into Dominic's hesitation. Let's dig into his internal conflict and show how his behavior begins to shift, setting the stage for the growing tension between him and Vanessa.

CHAPTER FIVE

Dominic sat in his car, the soft hum of the engine filling the silence as he stared at his phone. The text to Vanessa sat on the screen, sent and unanswered, but that wasn't what made him uneasy.

It was her words from the night before.

You're different. You make me feel safe.

The way she'd said it, soft and sincere, had hit him harder than he cared to admit. He should've been flattered. Hell, any other guy would've been thrilled. But all Dominic felt was pressure—an invisible weight settling on his chest.

Different? Safe? He wasn't that guy. He wasn't the guy you trusted with your heart. He was the guy you had fun with, the guy who made you laugh but never stayed long enough to get serious.

Vanessa wasn't like the others, though. She wasn't playing games or trying to prove something. She was real—too real. And that scared the hell out of him.

Dominic ran a hand over his face, leaning back in the driver's seat. He thought back to their dates, the way she looked at him like he was someone worth believing in. He didn't deserve that kind of faith.

He couldn't even remember the last time he'd let anyone get close enough to see the parts of him he kept hidden. The parts that told him he wasn't enough.

The text he'd sent that morning was just the first step. *Busy day ahead, but thinking of you.* It was his way of keeping her at a distance without cutting her off completely. But the thought of seeing her tonight—of seeing that look in her eyes that told him she believed in him—made his stomach tighten.

When Vanessa texted later that afternoon, asking if he wanted to come over for dinner, Dominic stared at the screen for longer than he cared to admit.

Can't tonight. Got a lot on my plate.

The excuse was easy, believable. But as soon as he hit send, the guilt crept in. Vanessa didn't press, just replied with a simple, *No problem. Hope your day gets better.*

Her kindness only made it worse.

The next day, Dominic joined Sean and Malik at the court, hoping a good game of basketball would clear his head. But even as he landed shot after shot, the knot in his chest didn't loosen.

"You good, man?" Sean asked during a break, tossing Dominic a water bottle.

"I'm fine," Dominic replied, avoiding eye contact.

Sean smirked. "You've been off lately. Don't tell me Vanessa's got you twisted."

Dominic rolled his eyes, taking a long sip of water. "It's not like that."

"Sure it's not," Sean said, but his tone was light. "Just don't overthink it, bro. If she's good for you, let her be good for you."

Dominic didn't respond.

By the end of the week, Vanessa couldn't ignore the change in Dominic's behavior. Their texts were shorter, their calls less frequent. He'd canceled their last two plans, and when she suggested dinner on Friday, he told her he was busy.

At first, she chalked it up to stress. Everyone had rough weeks. But as she sat on her couch scrolling through their old text conversations, she couldn't shake the feeling that something was wrong.

What changed?

She opened their latest conversation, re-reading his last message. *Sorry, just swamped lately. Rain check?*

Vanessa sighed, setting her phone down. She didn't want to push, but she also wasn't the type to sit back and wonder.

Later that night, Dominic found himself pacing his apartment, replaying the past few weeks in his head. Every time he thought about Vanessa, his chest tightened. She deserved better—someone who could meet her where she was. Someone who didn't run the second things started to get real.

But walking away wasn't easy, either. He liked Vanessa. He liked her more than he wanted to admit. And that was the problem.

As the clock ticked past midnight, Dominic grabbed his phone and opened their conversation. His thumb hovered over the keyboard, but no words came.

He tossed the phone onto the couch, frustration bubbling to the surface.

What the hell is wrong with me?

CHAPTER SIX

Vanessa stared at the text thread again, her thumb hovering over the keyboard. She'd typed *Hey, just checking in* three times, only to delete it each time.

It wasn't that she didn't notice the distance growing between them—she noticed. But something inside her told her not to chase after him.

She closed the app and set her phone down, letting out a soft sigh. *If he wants to talk, he will,* she told herself.

Vanessa wasn't the type to beg for attention or force someone to open up. She'd been there before, chasing after people who didn't want to be caught, and she'd promised herself she'd never do it again.

Still, it didn't stop the ache in her chest every time she thought about him.

The following days passed in a blur, with Dominic's texts becoming even more sporadic. Vanessa kept herself busy—lesson planning, catching up with friends, anything to distract herself.

Tiana noticed the shift during their next coffee date.

"You've been quiet lately," Tiana said, stirring her caramel macchiato. "What's going on with you and Dominic?"

Vanessa hesitated, swirling the foam in her latte with her spoon. "I'm not sure. He's been distant."

Tiana frowned. "Did something happen?"

"No, not really," Vanessa said, forcing a smile. "He's probably just busy. I don't want to read too much into it."

Tiana leaned back, studying her. "You're not the type to overthink. If you're feeling off, there's probably a reason."

Vanessa shrugged. "Maybe. But I'm not going to push. If he wants to talk, he'll talk."

For Dominic, the distance wasn't just about Vanessa—it was about what she represented. Every time he thought about her, he felt that familiar panic creeping in.

One night, as he sat on his couch scrolling aimlessly through social media, her name popped up in his notifications. She'd tagged him in a photo from one of their earlier dates—a simple snapshot of them laughing over ice cream cones.

His chest tightened as he stared at the picture. She looked so happy, so carefree. And all he could think about was how much he didn't deserve her.

Without thinking, Dominic untagged himself from the photo.

The next morning, Vanessa checked her notifications and frowned when she saw the change. Her heart sank, but she told herself not to jump to conclusions.

She sat with it for a while, replaying their time together in her head. There were so many good moments, so many things that felt real. But now, as she looked back, she couldn't ignore the signs—the way he'd always deflected her questions, the way he seemed to withdraw whenever things got too close.

Vanessa wasn't angry, just...sad. She'd opened herself up to him in a way she hadn't in a long time, and now it felt like she was watching something slip away without knowing why.

That evening, as she sat on her couch with a glass of wine, Vanessa finally let herself admit what she'd been avoiding.

He's pulling away.

The thought hurt more than she expected, but it also brought a strange sense of clarity. She wasn't going to chase him. If Dominic wanted out, she'd let him go.

Vanessa grabbed her phone and typed out a short message:

Hey, I've noticed you've been distant. If you need space, I understand. Just let me know where we stand.

She hesitated before hitting send, then set the phone down and waited.

CHAPTER SEVEN

Vanessa stared at her phone, the screen dimming after hours without a response. She'd sent the message, laid her feelings bare, and still…nothing.

By the time Dominic's reply finally came, it was late, and it wasn't much of an answer.

Sorry, been swamped. Talk soon.

Vanessa exhaled slowly, her heart sinking. She didn't bother replying. Deep down, she knew the truth—there wasn't going to be a "talk." Dominic wasn't swamped. He wasn't too busy. He was pulling away, and now she had to decide how much longer she was willing to wait for someone who didn't seem to want to be found.

With a shaky breath, Vanessa closed her messages and turned off her phone.

Dominic, on the other hand, barely gave the message a second thought. As far as he was concerned, he'd done his part by responding, even if it wasn't much.

The truth was, he didn't want to face Vanessa's questions or her disappointment. He didn't want to face anything at all.

Instead, he did what he always did—he went out.

The bar was loud and packed, the kind of place Dominic hadn't planned on being that night. But sitting alone in his apartment had felt unbearable, so here he was, sipping on his second whiskey neat and pretending the noise didn't bother him.

She found him before he even realized he was looking.

"Drinking alone?" she asked, sliding onto the stool beside him with a confident smile.

Dominic turned, his gaze sweeping over her bold red lipstick and the curve of her smile. “Not anymore.”

The conversation was light, playful, and meaningless—exactly what he needed. He didn’t catch her name, and he didn’t ask. They shared a few drinks, exchanged a few laughs, and when the night ended, they went their separate ways.

As Dominic walked out of the bar, her number scrawled on a napkin in his pocket, he felt the emptiness creeping back in. The distraction had worked for a while, but now it was gone, and the silence returned.

On to the next, he thought, shoving the napkin into his pocket.

CHAPTER EIGHT

Brittany wasn't looking for love, but she wasn't ruling it out, either. She was the kind of person who took life as it came—spontaneous, vibrant, and always ready for the next adventure.

Dominic met her at Malik's party, and from the moment they started talking, it was clear they clicked.

"You're Dominic, right?" she said, leaning against the kitchen counter with a drink in hand.

"That's me," Dominic replied, flashing his signature grin.

"Malik says you're trouble."

Dominic smirked. "Only if you're not paying attention."

Their connection was effortless, full of playful banter and shared laughs. For Dominic, it was easy. Brittany wasn't asking for too much—just someone to share the moment with. And for a while, that was enough.

But Brittany, for all her laid-back charm, couldn't help but hope for more.

"You're fun," she said one night as they shared a late-night burger at a diner.

Dominic grinned, wiping ketchup from the corner of his mouth. "I get that a lot."

Brittany rolled her eyes, laughing. "I mean it, though. I like spending time with you."

"Good," Dominic replied, leaning back in the booth. "Because I like spending time with you too."

But his words didn't carry the weight Brittany was hoping for, and deep down, she knew it.

One Saturday afternoon, Brittany had convinced Dominic to join her at a farmer's market. It wasn't his usual scene, but something about her enthusiasm made it hard to say no.

"This is the best spot for fresh lemonade," Brittany said, tugging his arm toward a small stand decorated with sunflowers.

Dominic chuckled, letting her pull him along. "You seem pretty passionate about lemonade."

"Only because it's amazing," she said, handing him a cup with a grin. "Trust me."

He took a sip, raising an eyebrow. "Okay, I'll give you this one. It's good."

"See? I told you," Brittany said, nudging him playfully.

They spent the rest of the afternoon wandering through the stalls, sampling pastries and joking about the outrageous prices of handmade candles. For a moment, Dominic let himself relax, caught up in Brittany's light and easy energy.

As the weeks went on, Dominic kept things light—always joking, always deflecting when the conversation got too serious.

One night, as they sat on her couch watching a movie, Brittany decided to test the waters.

"What are you looking for, Dominic?" she asked casually, her eyes on the screen.

"What do you mean?"

"I mean...this," Brittany said, gesturing between them. "Are we just having fun, or is there something more?"

Dominic hesitated for a split second before answering. "I think we're doing fine as we are. Don't you?"

Brittany's smile faltered, but she quickly masked it with a laugh. "Yeah, sure."

But her laughter didn't reach her eyes, and Dominic noticed.

From that point on, the dynamic shifted. Brittany started pulling back slightly, testing whether Dominic would notice.

He noticed, but he didn't act. Instead, he told himself it was for the best.

One evening, as they sat in her car after a casual dinner, Brittany finally decided she'd had enough.

"You know, Dominic," she said, turning to face him. "I thought you were different."

Dominic frowned. "What's that supposed to mean?"

"It means I thought this could be something, but I see now that it's not," Brittany said, her tone calm but resolute. "And that's fine. But I can't keep pretending this is enough for me when it's not."

Dominic opened his mouth to respond, but nothing came out.

"I like you, Dominic," Brittany continued. "But I need more than this."

"Brittany—"

"It's okay," she interrupted, giving him a small smile. "Really. I hope you find what you're looking for."

With that, she opened the door and stepped out, leaving Dominic alone in the car.

Dominic sat in the silence, staring at the spot where Brittany had just been. He didn't feel heartbroken—he never let himself get close enough to feel that way. But her words lingered in his mind, sharp and unrelenting.

I need more than this.

He didn't drive home right away. Instead, he sat there for a long time, the weight of her disappointment settling over him like a heavy fog.

And yet, when the silence became too much, he did what he always did—he buried it.

CHAPTER NINE

Dominic had been to enough parties to know what to expect—the same music, the same drinks, the same faces. But this one felt different the moment she walked in.

Veronica didn't just enter a room; she commanded it. Her confidence was palpable, her gaze sharp as it swept across the crowd. Unlike the other women who vied for attention, she didn't seem to care who noticed her.

"Who's that?" Dominic muttered to Malik, nodding toward her.

"Veronica," Malik replied, smirking. "Word of advice—don't bother."

"Why not?"

"She doesn't fall for the games, man. She's on another level."

Dominic grinned, intrigued. "You know I love a challenge."

Veronica was standing by the drink table, swirling her glass of red wine as if she had all the time in the world.

"Not much of a party, is it?" Dominic said, sidling up beside her.

Veronica glanced at him, her expression unreadable. "That depends. Are you about to make it worse or better?"

Dominic chuckled. "Guess we'll find out."

Her lips curled into a faint smile, but she didn't give him much else.

"You're not like most people here," Dominic continued, leaning casually against the table.

"And you've figured that out already?" she replied, raising an eyebrow.

Dominic shrugged, flashing his signature grin. "Just an observation."

"Hmm," Veronica said, taking a sip of her wine. "Observations are easy. Substance is harder."

For the first time in years, Dominic felt like he was the one being tested—and he liked it.

Over the next few days, Dominic couldn't get Veronica out of his head. Her confidence, her mystery—everything about her was magnetic.

When he finally worked up the nerve to text her, she didn't respond right away. Hours passed before a simple reply came through: *Busy. Maybe later.*

The "maybe" stung more than he wanted to admit, but it also made him try harder.

When Veronica finally agreed to meet him for coffee, Dominic made sure everything was perfect. He arrived early, snagging the best table and ordering her favorite drink—a detail he'd picked up during one of their brief conversations.

"You're trying too hard," Veronica said as she slid into the seat across from him.

Dominic laughed, unbothered. "And yet, here you are."

Veronica smirked, taking a sip of her drink. "Don't get used to it."

Despite her cool demeanor, the conversation flowed easily. Veronica had a way of making Dominic feel like he was peeling back layers, even if he wasn't sure what lay beneath.

After their first date, Dominic was hooked. He texted her often, planned thoughtful outings, and did everything he could to show her he was serious.

Veronica, however, remained elusive.

"You're hard to pin down," Dominic said one night as they walked through the park.

"That's by design," Veronica replied, glancing at him with a faint smile.

"Afraid I'll figure you out?"

"Maybe I'm afraid you won't," she said, her tone teasing but distant.

Dominic didn't know what to make of her words, but they only made him want her more.

For every effort Dominic made, Veronica responded with just enough to keep him invested. She'd call him unexpectedly, show up at his apartment with dinner, or lean in close during their conversations, her touch lingering just a moment too long.

"You're different," Dominic said one evening as they sat on his couch, sharing a bottle of wine.

"Good different, I hope," Veronica replied, her voice smooth.

Dominic nodded, his eyes fixed on hers. "The best kind."

Veronica smiled but didn't respond, letting the silence stretch just long enough for Dominic to believe she agreed.

By the time Veronica introduced Dominic to her friends, he was already imagining a future with her.

"She's got you whipped," Sean joked after meeting her.

"Whatever, man," Dominic replied, grinning. "She's amazing."

And in his mind, she was. Veronica had become the center of his world, the person he thought about when he woke up and the last person he texted before going to bed.

CHAPTER TEN

The cabin was nestled in the mountains, surrounded by towering pines and the kind of stillness that made the city feel like a distant memory. Dominic had been looking forward to this trip since Veronica suggested it, and now that they were here, everything felt...perfect.

Their first night was filled with easy conversation and laughter. Veronica had insisted on cooking dinner—a simple pasta dish that filled the cabin with warmth and the comforting aroma of garlic and herbs.

"You're full of surprises," Dominic said as he poured them both glasses of wine.

"Why's that?" Veronica asked, glancing up from the stove.

"I didn't peg you as the cooking type," Dominic teased.

"Don't get used to it," Veronica replied with a smirk. "This is a rare occasion."

After dinner, they sat by the fire, the room illuminated by the soft glow of the flames.

"This is what life should feel like," Dominic said, leaning back in his chair.

Veronica glanced at him, her expression unreadable. "Moments like this are nice," she said simply.

Dominic wanted to ask her what she meant, but something in her tone made him hesitate. Instead, he reached for her hand, and for once, she didn't pull away.

The next morning, they set off on a hiking trail Veronica had found online.

“You sure you can keep up?” Veronica teased as they climbed the steep incline.

Dominic laughed. “Are you kidding? I’ll be at the top before you even notice.”

They reached the summit just as the sun began to peek through the clouds, bathing the mountains in a soft golden light.

“It’s beautiful,” Veronica said, her voice quieter than usual.

“So are you,” Dominic said without thinking.

Veronica turned to him, her expression softening for a brief moment. “You’re something else, Dominic.”

That night, Dominic couldn’t sleep. Veronica had fallen asleep beside him, her breathing steady and calm. He watched her for a long time, marveling at how effortless she made everything seem.

She’s the one, he thought to himself. *I have to make this official.*

On the drive back to the city, Dominic felt more certain than ever. They were silent for most of the trip, but it wasn’t an uncomfortable silence. For Dominic, it felt like the kind of quiet you could only share with someone who truly understood you.

As he helped Veronica carry her bag to her car, he smiled. “Thanks for the trip. It was...everything.”

Veronica gave him a faint smile. “I’m glad you enjoyed it.”

When she drove off, Dominic was already planning the next step.

A week later, Dominic decided it was time. They were sitting on his couch, a half-empty bottle of wine between them, when he turned to her.

“I’ve been thinking,” Dominic started, his voice steady.

“Uh-oh,” Veronica teased, raising an eyebrow. “That sounds serious.”

“It is,” Dominic said, smiling nervously. “I want us to be exclusive.”

Veronica’s smile faltered slightly, but she quickly recovered. “Exclusive?”

"Yeah," Dominic said, leaning forward. "I don't want to see anyone else. I just want to be with you."

Veronica leaned back, her expression unreadable. "That's...unexpected."

"Unexpected how?" Dominic asked, his confidence wavering.

"I mean, we've been having fun," Veronica said carefully. "I didn't realize you were thinking about labels."

Dominic frowned, his heart sinking. "Is that a bad thing?"

Veronica hesitated, choosing her words carefully. "It's not bad, Dominic. It's just...not what I want."

"What do you mean?"

"I mean, I'm not looking for exclusivity. I like what we have, but I don't want to put a label on it."

Dominic felt his chest tighten. "So you don't see this going anywhere?"

"Dominic," Veronica said softly, "we're just enjoying each other's company. Isn't that enough?"

"No, it's not," Dominic said, his voice cracking slightly. "At least, not for me."

"We should call it a night," Veronica said softly, standing up and grabbing her coat.

Dominic stood as well, his heart racing. "Veronica, wait."

She paused, glancing back at him with an unreadable expression.

"What is it, Dominic?" she asked, her tone calm but distant.

"I just..." He struggled for the right words, his throat tightening. "I don't want this to end like this."

Veronica looked at him for a moment, her face unreadable. Then she turned toward the door. "I have to go."

Without another word, she walked out, closing the door behind her with a soft click that felt louder than any slam.

Dominic stood there, frozen, his chest tight and his thoughts racing. The silence that followed was suffocating, and for the first time, he didn't know what to do.

He wandered back to the couch, staring at the wine glass she'd left on the table. Picking it up, he turned it over in his hands, the faint lipstick smudge catching the light.

He thought about rinsing it out, but something stopped him. Instead, he set it gently in the sink, leaving it there for days.

Weeks later, the glass was clean and back in the cabinet, but the memory of her lipstick on the rim lingered like a stubborn shadow.

CHAPTER ELEVEN

After Veronica left, Dominic sat in silence, his thoughts racing. The wine glass she'd left on the table felt like a metaphor for everything—unfinished, empty, and out of reach.

For the first time, Dominic felt the sting of rejection. He'd always been the one to keep things light, the one to walk away, the one in control. But now, the tables had turned, and he didn't know how to handle it.

He picked up his phone, staring at her number. His fingers hovered over the screen before he tossed the phone aside.

"Give her space," he muttered to himself. "She'll come around."

But deep down, he wasn't so sure.

A few days later, Sean called Dominic up.

"Yo, what's up?" Dominic answered, trying to sound casual.

"Nothing much," Sean said. "Just wanted to check in. You doing okay?"

"Yeah, why wouldn't I be?"

Sean hesitated. "Look, man, I wasn't going to say anything, but Tiana and I were out at dinner the other night, and we saw Veronica."

"Okay," Dominic said slowly, his chest tightening.

"She wasn't alone," Sean added.

Dominic's stomach dropped. "What do you mean?"

"She was with some guy," Sean said. "I didn't want to assume anything, but they seemed...close."

There was a long pause before Dominic spoke. "You're sure it was her?"

"Positive," Sean said. "Tiana even took a quick video. I wasn't going to show you, but I thought you should know."

Later that evening, Sean sent Dominic the video. It was short, just a few seconds of Veronica laughing and leaning in close to a man at the table. The way she looked at him—comfortable, confident, and carefree—made Dominic's stomach churn.

He replayed the clip a few times, each time feeling the sting of her rejection all over again.

When Dominic told Malik about the video, Malik shook his head. "I told you, man. Veronica doesn't do attachments. This is just who she is."

Dominic frowned. "You think she's been seeing him this whole time?"

Malik shrugged. "Does it matter? She was never yours to begin with. Don't waste your time chasing someone who isn't chasing you back."

Dominic leaned back, his head in his hands. "I thought it was different."

"I know you did," Malik said. "But take this as a lesson, Dom. You've been on the other side of this enough times to know how it feels now. Don't let it break you—learn from it."

After the video, Dominic tried texting Veronica once, a simple, "Hey, can we talk?"

She never responded. Days turned into weeks, and Dominic came to accept what he already knew: Veronica was gone.

For the first time in his life, Dominic felt the emptiness he'd left in so many others. And he couldn't run from it.

CHAPTER TWELVE

For the first time in a long while, Dominic had nowhere to be and no one to call. The stillness was suffocating. He sat on the couch, his head tilted back against the cushion, staring at the ceiling. The TV flickered in the background, paused on the same screen for hours, but he hadn't noticed.

Veronica's rejection replayed in his mind like a song he couldn't stop humming. The way she had walked out without looking back, the way her words had felt final—it all lingered, a cruel reminder of what he thought they had.

Dominic leaned back, closing his eyes, but the silence grew louder. For years, he had filled every moment with noise—parties, dates, flirty texts, casual hookups. Anything to keep from being alone.

Now, with no one to distract him, the weight of his choices hit him like a tidal wave.

Why do I do this?

The question came unbidden, catching Dominic off guard. He tried to brush it aside, but it clung to him, demanding an answer.

He thought about Vanessa and how he'd ghosted her without a second thought. About Brittany, who had tried to connect with him but was met with walls he wasn't ready to tear down. And now Veronica—Veronica, who had never truly been his, no matter how much he tried to convince himself otherwise.

Dominic's mind drifted to his younger self, a boy sitting on the steps of his childhood home, watching his parents argue through the screen door.

His father's words echoed faintly in his mind: "You don't let anyone get too close. That's how you stay in control."

At the time, Dominic hadn't understood what his father meant. But as he grew older, he started to see it in his actions. His dad never let anyone see him sweat, never admitted when something hurt. To Dominic, it looked like strength.

Maybe that's why I never let anyone in, Dominic thought. *Because I thought that's what men do.*

But then another memory surfaced—one he'd buried for years. He was sixteen, sitting on the bleachers after school, waiting for a girl named Bailey.

She'd been the first person he'd ever opened up to, the first person he thought might actually understand him. He'd waited for hours that day, but she never showed.

The next morning, he found out she'd been with someone else.

Dominic felt his chest tighten as the memory came rushing back. He remembered the shame, the embarrassment, the anger. He swore that day he'd never let himself be that vulnerable again.

And I haven't, he realized.

Dominic stood up, pacing the room. His reflection in the window caught his eye, and for the first time, he didn't look away.

"You're scared," he muttered to himself. "You've been scared your whole life."

The words hung in the air, heavy and undeniable.

He thought about Veronica, how she'd mirrored his own behavior back at him. She had been distant, unattached, unwilling to let him get too close—just like he'd been with Vanessa and Brittany.

Is this what it feels like to be on the other side?

Dominic sat back down, his head in his hands. He didn't have all the answers, but for the first time, he felt like he was asking the right questions.

What if this isn't who I have to be?

The thought scared him as much as it gave him hope.

CHAPTER THIRTEEN

Dominic's reflection in the mirror had become a stranger. For days, he'd been staring at himself, turning over everything Malik said and everything he'd uncovered about his past.

It wasn't just Veronica. It wasn't just Angela. It was every moment in between—the walls he'd built, the excuses he'd made, and the pain he'd caused.

Now, for the first time, he realized he couldn't keep running.

The thought of apologizing made his stomach churn, but he couldn't ignore it. He thought about Vanessa first—the way she had looked at him, hopeful, until he ghosted her without explanation.

He picked up his phone, scrolling through old contacts until her name popped up.

What do I even say? he thought, his finger hovering over the call button.

Finally, he typed out a message.

Hey Vanessa, it's Dominic. I know this is out of the blue, but I need to talk to you. If you're willing, let me know. If not, I understand.

His thumb hovered over the send button for what felt like an eternity before he pressed it.

The hours that followed felt endless. Dominic kept checking his phone, half-hoping she wouldn't respond and half-praying she would.

When her reply came, his heart raced:

I'll hear you out. When and where?

Dominic met Vanessa at a quiet café, arriving early to ensure they'd have privacy. When she walked in, her expression was guarded, her posture stiff.

He stood awkwardly as she approached, motioning to the chair across from him. She sat without saying a word, her eyes fixed on him expectantly.

"Vanessa," Dominic started, his voice softer than usual. "Thank you for coming. I know I don't deserve this."

Vanessa crossed her arms, her eyes sharp but curious. "I'm still figuring out why I even agreed. So, talk."

Dominic took a deep breath, the weight of his own emotions pressing on his chest. "I owe you more than an apology. What I did to you...it was cruel. I didn't give you a reason. I didn't give you anything. I just left. And I've thought about that a lot lately."

Vanessa's brow furrowed slightly, but she didn't interrupt.

"I was selfish," Dominic continued. "I didn't know how to handle someone like you—someone kind, patient, and willing to care for me in a way I wasn't ready to accept. I didn't know how to let you in because I was terrified of what it might mean if I did. I've spent my whole life running from people who tried to care about me, and you didn't deserve to be on the receiving end of that."

He looked up, meeting her eyes. "And now, after going through what I put you through, I understand what it feels like. To care about someone, to think there's something real, only for them to disappear without a word. It broke me, Vanessa. And it made me realize how much I've hurt people—how much I hurt you."

Vanessa leaned back, her expression softening but still cautious. "So, what do you want from me, Dominic? Forgiveness? Closure?"

"No," Dominic said quickly. "I don't expect anything from you. I just needed to say this. To tell you that what I did wasn't your fault. You weren't too much or not enough. You were exactly what I needed, but I wasn't strong enough to see it then. And I'm sorry."

Vanessa's lips pressed into a thin line, her fingers tracing the edge of her coffee cup. "You're right—you were selfish. You left me questioning everything, Dominic. Wondering if I did something wrong or if I wasn't good enough. Do you know how much that messes with someone?"

Dominic nodded, his throat tightening. "I do now. And I hate that I made you feel that way. You didn't deserve it."

Vanessa sighed, her eyes glistening with unshed tears. "Hearing this doesn't undo the past, but...it helps. I needed to hear it."

As Vanessa stood to leave, Dominic rose too. "Thank you for letting me say this," he said. "And for hearing me out. I'll never forgive myself for how I treated you, but I hope...I hope you find someone who sees you for everything you are and treats you the way you deserve."

Vanessa paused, her gaze steady. "I already have. But thank you, Dominic. I hope you find peace, too."

As she walked away, Dominic sat back down, a mix of relief and regret washing over him. The apology hadn't erased the past, but it had given him something he hadn't had before—a chance to take accountability.

CHAPTER FOURTEEN

The café felt quieter as Dominic sat alone, his coffee growing cold in front of him. Vanessa had been gone for twenty minutes, but her words lingered like a melody he couldn't shake.

"You left me questioning everything, Dominic. Wondering if I did something wrong or if I wasn't good enough."

She hadn't said it to hurt him—he could tell by her tone—but the truth of it hit him like a brick. He had done that to her, and likely to so many others.

For so long, he had believed closure was a single moment, a conversation, an apology. Now he realized it was a process—one that didn't end with words, but with action.

Back at his apartment, Dominic sat on his couch, his phone in hand. He scrolled through his contacts until he found Brittany's name.

What do I even say?

With a deep breath, he typed out a message:

Hey Brittany, it's Dominic. I've been doing a lot of thinking, and I owe you an apology. If you're willing to meet, I'd really like to talk. If not, I understand.

He hit send before he could second-guess himself and set the phone down, the nerves settling in his chest like a weight.

The coffee shop was a familiar place, though Dominic hadn't been there in months. Brittany had chosen the table in the corner, away from the crowd, and was already seated when he arrived.

"Brittany," Dominic said, his voice steady but nervous as he sat across from her.

"Dominic," she replied coolly, leaning back in her chair. "You said you wanted to talk, so talk."

Dominic took a deep breath, clasping his hands on the table. "I'm not even sure where to start," he admitted. "But I owe you more than an apology. What I did to you...it was cruel. I didn't give you a reason. I didn't give you anything. I just left. And I've thought about that a lot lately."

"You mean you disappeared," Brittany corrected, her tone sharp. "You didn't just leave, Dominic. You ghosted me. Like I didn't matter."

Dominic nodded, his throat tightening. "You're right. I ghosted you, and it wasn't fair. I was distant, unavailable, and when you tried to call me out on it, I shut down instead of stepping up. I didn't know how to handle someone like you—someone who saw through me, who wasn't afraid to call me out."

"And why should that have been my problem?" Brittany asked, her voice rising slightly. "You were scared, so I had to deal with the fallout? I deserved better than that, Dominic. I deserved someone who wasn't going to treat me like I was disposable."

"You're right," Dominic said quietly. "You did deserve better. And I'm sorry I couldn't be that for you. I was selfish and immature, and I wasn't ready to be with someone who knew her worth."

Brittany leaned forward, her eyes narrowing. "You made me doubt myself. I thought, maybe if I had been less direct, less honest about what I wanted, you wouldn't have left. But now I see it wasn't about me at all. It was about you not knowing how to handle someone who wouldn't settle for your bare minimum."

Dominic looked down, her words cutting deeper than he expected. "You're right. It wasn't about you. It was about me being too scared to face what I was feeling."

Brittany sighed, leaning back in her chair. "Hearing this doesn't fix things, Dominic. But...it helps. At least now, I know it wasn't my fault."

Dominic nodded, his voice steady but soft. "It never was. And I'm sorry I made you feel that way."

As Brittany stood to leave, she paused. "I hope you figure it out. And don't do to anyone else what you did to me."

Dominic sat at the table long after Brittany left, the echo of her words swirling in his mind.

"Don't do to anyone else what you did to me."

It wasn't forgiveness, but it wasn't rejection either. It was a truth he would carry with him, a reminder of how far he still had to go.

For so long, Dominic had believed closure was a single moment, a conversation, an apology. Now he realized it was a process—one that didn't end with words, but with action.

He didn't know what came next, but for the first time, he felt like he was starting to figure it out.

FINAL CHAPTER: OPEN ENDS

Dominic stood on the balcony of his apartment that evening, the city lights stretching out before him.

The quiet felt different now—not oppressive, but calm. He let the cool night air wash over him, his thoughts turning to everything that had brought him to this moment.

Vanessa's guarded forgiveness. Brittany's sharp honesty. Malik's tough love. And Veronica—the woman who had held a mirror to him and forced him to see himself for what he truly was.

He wasn't healed. He wasn't whole. But he was trying.

As the night deepened, Dominic took a deep breath, feeling the weight of the past still clinging to him, but lighter somehow.

"Maybe someday," he thought, *"I'll be someone worth forgiving."*

AFTERWORD

Dominic's story in *The Reverse Game* is not about a perfect transformation. It's about the messy, uncertain process of confronting who you've been and choosing, every day, to try to be better.

For years, Dominic ran from his fears, his emotions, and the people who cared for him. It took heartbreak and honesty to stop him in his tracks and force him to see the damage he'd left behind—not just in others, but in himself.

There is no clean ending to a journey like this. Forgiveness doesn't come quickly, and healing doesn't happen overnight. But Dominic's story reminds us that change is possible, even for those who think it's too late.

Whether he finds redemption, forgiveness, or peace is up to him. And maybe that's the most hopeful thing of all—that it's not about where you've been, but where you're willing to go.

Made in the USA
Middletown, DE
28 November 2024

65324919R00027